2015 First printing

Kristoph and the First Christmas Tree

Text copyright © 2015 by Claudia Cangilla McAdam
Illustrations copyright © 2015 by Dave Hill

ISBN 978-1-61261-630-8

The Paraclete Press name and logo (dove on cross) are trademarks of Paraclete Press, Inc.

Library of Congress Cataloging-in-Publication Data
McAdam, Claudia Cangilla.
  Kristoph and the first Christmas tree / Claudia Cangilla McAdam ; illustrated by David Hill.
    pages cm
  ISBN 978-1-61261-630-8 (hardback)
  1. Boniface, Saint, Archbishop of Mainz, approximately 675-754—Juvenile literature. 2. Christian saints—Europe—
Biography—Juvenile literature. I. Hill, David (David M.), illustrator. II. Title.
  BX4700.B7M33 2015
  270.2092—dc23   2015018300

10 9 8 7 6 5 4 3 2 1

Published by Paraclete Press
Brewster, Massachusetts
www.paracletepress.com

Printed in Malaysia

With love for my grandson Christopher,
who fills me with happiness and hope
—C.C.M.

To Anne, David and Amy
—D.H.

Germany, December 24, 722

areful, Kit. You don't want to slice off your fingers."

Boniface, the priest, smiled and ruffled the boy's hair.

Kristoph stopped sharpening the ax. He liked being

called "Kit." He'd never had a nickname in the orphanage.

Mostly, he was just called "boy."

"Daylight is fading, and the snow is starting," the priest said. "We'd best leave now if we want to reach the village by nightfall."

Kristoph wrapped the ax head with a hide and tied it with a thin leather strip. He shoved the handle through his rope belt. Into his bag he dropped a candle rolled of coarse beeswax and some hard biscuits wrapped in a cloth. They would eat their dinner, such as it was, by candlelight. Probably in a barn in the village, but he didn't care. This was his first Christmas spent outside the orphanage.

They picked their way through the forest, the silver light of late afternoon sifting through the evergreen trees and softly kissing the falling snow. As they crested a hill, the priest thrust out his arm, stopping Kristoph.

In the valley below, a dozen men circled a huge tree. A boy stood nearby, a frayed rope knotted around his wrists.

"Pagans," Boniface murmured. The men's chanting swept to them on an icy gust of wind. "That oak is sacred to them."

Kristoph pointed at the boy. "Who's that?"

"The son of the village chieftain."

"What are those men going to do to him?" Kristoph asked, his eyes as big and brown as mincemeat pies.

Boniface stroked his beard and narrowed his eyes. "Nothing good, I fear. Come."

They strode into the clearing, and the men quit chanting. The group turned toward Boniface, and Kristoph ducked behind the priest's robes.

The largest man reached them in three swift steps. His hair and beard framed his face in inky blackness. Thick eyebrows reminded Kristoph of horns.

"Come to convert us, have you, priest?" Chapped lips spread to reveal yellow teeth, several of which were missing.

"I heard you preaching in the village last week," he growled.

"Seems you weren't listening." Boniface nodded at the oak. "You choose to worship a tree rather than the one, true God."

"Why not?"

The priest smiled, spread his arms, and gently shrugged his shoulders. "Because it has no power. Only God does."

A laugh roared from the man. "Prove it!"

"Through God's power, I shall fell your sacred tree with one ax stroke," Boniface said. The men snickered; their young prisoner's face grew as gray as the dusky sky. "Kit?"

Kristoph pulled the ax from his belt. Its head was no bigger than a man's hand. He glanced at the massive oak. If his arms hugged the trunk, his fingers wouldn't come close to touching. "One stroke?" he asked.

"Faith, child," the priest whispered. He made the sign of the cross, touching forehead, chest, and each shoulder in turn.

He lifted the ax, and with one mighty whack, the blade split the bark. A huge crack ate its way through the trunk. The tree tilted and teetered, then toppled to the ground in what sounded like a clap of thunder.

The men stared, open-mouthed. Kristoph did, too. In the stump of the felled oak, a fir tree as tall as a man quivered in the quake. Had it been there all along, tucked behind the gigantic tree? Or did it spring from the base of the oak itself?

Boniface drew his fingers along a branch of the evergreen. "This child of the forest is the wood of peace. See how it points toward heaven?" The men's eyes lifted skyward. "It is the sign of endless life, for its branches are ever green. Let this be called the tree of the Christ Child. Gather around it, not in the wild woods, but in your homes. It shall not shelter evil deeds, but loving gifts and lights of kindness."

He raised the ax again, and with one more swing, he cut down the fir. Two of the men shouldered the tree. "Get thee home now," Boniface said. "Mend your lives. Beg forgiveness of our Lord on this, the eve of His birth." In silence the men melted into the forest.

Kristoph ripped the rope from the boy's wrists. "Thank you!" the boy cried. "You must come home with me. Father will want to thank you. Share our Christmas! Mother is roasting a goose and yams, and there are raisin cakes."

Boniface nodded, and Kristoph's stomach growled.

As he took back the ax, he spotted another fir, not quite his size, growing along the path. It took him three swings to chop it down. "For our Christmas," Kristoph said, as he knelt to tie the rope around the bottom branches.

He stood and followed the others, dragging the fir behind him along the way, tracing a path through the sprinkled-sugar snow. A sharp, sweet scent of evergreens wrapped them like a quilt as they trudged onward toward hearth and home, happiness and hope—

and a joyous celebration lit by a beeswax candle atop
a Christmas tree.

A Prayer of Blessing for a Christmas Tree

Based on the words of St. Boniface
by Claudia Cangilla McAdam

A

child

of the

earth, the

Christmas

tree, makes a

gift of itself, O

Lord, to thee.

Sign of endless life,

branches ever green,

wood of peace pointing

to heaven unseen. May it

give You honor; may You

shower Your grace upon faith-

ful people gathered in this place.

Amen.